Act Normal

And Don't Tell Anyone That

Christmas Is Early

By Christian Darkin

First Printing 2016 by Rational Stories
www.RationalStories.com

The illustrations are by the author but use some elements for which thanks and credits go to www.obsidiandawn.com, kuschelirmel- stock, Theshelfs and waywardgal at Deviantart.com
Story and illustrations by © Christian Darkin.

CHAPTER 1

I have been doing some Maths, and I think there is a big problem.

This spring, the first time I saw a bluebell flower in the wood was on April 14th. I know that because I wrote it down in my special book.

On the news they said that this was too early. They said that normally bluebells start to make flowers on May 5th. They said that they were early because the world is getting warmer. They said this was because of global warming and they said that this was a Big Problem.

Then on July 15th Dad took us blackberry picking and we made some jelly. It was nice, but the Internet said that blackberries do not usually come out until August and that this was because of Global Warming as well.

This year, I wrote in my book about conkers being early too, and butterflies.

This is all to do with Global Warming. The ice at the North Pole is melting and giving everything that lives there lots of problems.

Things living at the North Pole:
- polar bears

- seals
- Santa Claus

Everything is 21 days early this year, so if my Maths is right, this Christmas will be on 4th December.

This will be very bad. Nobody will have bought their Christmas presents or food and everyone will still be at school!

People in this story:

Me: I am Jenny. People often say, "Jenny's heart is in the right place." That means that I like to do good things and solve problems. But they only usually say it when my plans have not done exactly what I meant them to do.

Adam: My brother, Adam doesn't make plans. He just does whatever he thinks of as soon as he thinks of it. His heart is in the right place too, but people don't say so very often. They almost never say that he is a good little angel, but in this story, he really, really is.

Dad: Dad knows a lot of secrets. He has to decide which people to tell which secrets to, and that must be hard because strange things happen all the time, and it is important that the right people know the right secrets.

CHAPTER 2

I'm getting really sure now that Christmas is coming early.

Dad took Adam and me into town to do shopping, and EVERYTHING was Christmassy.

There were Christmas lights on all the lamp posts. All the shop windows had sparkly things and pretend snow in them, and there was even a big Santa Claus Grotto right in the middle of the town.

It was a big thing like a cave with tinsel and snow on the outside. I wanted to take a picture because we were making one for our school Christmas play, but Dad started walking really fast and pointed to a window on the other side of the street.

He said, "Look, Adam, Lego!"

I think he was trying to stop Adam seeing the grotto. Dad shook his head and said, "It's too early for all this!"

I said, "Yes, I know. It's global warming", but I don't think he was listening.

We went into the shop after Adam.

Dad said, "We are doing Christmas shopping. We're not going to look at toys."

That was a silly thing to say because there were lots of toys and they had a whole big section on dinosaurs and another big section on cars so Adam was never not going to look at them.

Anyway, I saw a big chemistry set and I said, "Can I have this for Christmas?"

Dad looked a bit scared. He said, "Do you remember what happened last time you played with chemicals, Jenny?"

I did remember because some of the trees in the wood are purple with blue leaves now, but that is in another story.

Dad said, "We're looking for something for Granny."

I looked around, but I couldn't see anything Granny might want. She doesn't do chemistry anymore. Also, I couldn't see much because there were lots and lots of people in the shop. Also, I couldn't see Adam.

"Adam? Adam?" said Dad. He couldn't see Adam either. We ran to the dinosaur section, then we ran to the cars section, then we ran to the jokes section, but he wasn't there.

Then we heard the shop's alarm going off, so we knew which way Adam had gone. It's good that shops have alarms. It means we always know when Adam has left a shop.

Dad grabbed me and we ran out of the shop. We still couldn't see Adam, but Dad made a guess.

Santa's Grotto had a little elf-sized fence around it, and people were lined up waiting to see Santa. Dad jumped over the fence, and pushed past the people. They looked angry.

(Pushing past people is rude, unless you're looking for Adam.)

We went inside. Adam was there.

Can you guess what he was doing?

CHAPTER 3

Adam was standing in front of Father Christmas, holding a big pile of boxes of toys. At the bottom, there was a big Lego box with a spaceship on it. In the middle, there was a game with plastic horses.

He was also holding a big lorry with lots of little cars inside it, a box full of dinosaurs and a big book for putting football trading cards in.

He was telling Santa about each toy and telling him which of Adam's friends he should give it to. Santa was looking a bit confused, and going, "He! He! He!"

This was because he was not the real Santa. He was a grotto Santa which is not the same thing. The real Santa goes, "Ho! Ho! Ho!" Everybody knows that.

Dad started telling Santa he was sorry, and telling Adam he was naughty at the same time, but it came out as, "I'm sorry, you're very naughty!" which is what's called a mixed message.

I was looking around the grotto. This grotto was made of a sort of plastic to keep the rain out. The one we were making at school was made of glue mixed with paper. I decided we would have to cover it in plastic bags to make it waterproof. (I am very glad I had that idea – you'll see why later.)

Dad took Adam by the hand and picked up the toys to take back to the shop. As we left, I said to Santa: "Are the ice-caps melting?"

He said, "Um..."

I said, "Are you going to be early this year like the blackberries?"

He just looked confused and went, "He! He! He!" again, because he wasn't the real Santa.

I was just going to ask how he got to every house in the world in one night (I had done some maths about that and it's very hard), but he said; "Have you been naughty or nice this year?"

That's a very hard question because you do a lot of things in a whole year. Some of them are naughty but end up nice (like the purple trees with blue leaves) and some of them are supposed to be nice, but end up naughty (like the zombie robots I made).

I didn't really know how to answer him.

CHAPTER 4

I asked the Internet about things being early, and it said that the world is warming up because of pollution and the ice caps at the North Pole and South Pole are melting.

This is why everything is early, and Christmas will be all messed up because Santa will get here on 4th December, and nobody will have got their presents, and people will forget to leave out mince pies for him. They might even still have their fires lit, so he will burn his bum when he comes down the chimney.

To solve this problem, I decided to make a new ice-cap. An ice-cap is just a place with lots of ice in it so, I thought, that should be easy.

I have an atlas - which is a big book of maps of the world. I decided that good places for new ice caps are:

- Canada – because it is close to the old one.
- Egypt – because it is too hot there and it would be nice for them to have more water.

and

- our school library – because it is easy to get to, and because it is already very cold in there.

I decided our school library was best because I could get my friends at school to help. Also, if we did it in the Maths section, it would be right at the back, and there is a door into a cupboard with pipes in it. The ice cap can go back into there. Also nobody goes into the Maths section much except me, so nobody would find our ice-cap as long as we all just Acted Normal.

I sent an email to my friends:

Dear Everybody,

The North Pole is melting, so Santa will get all confused and come on 4th December this year. We can fix this by making a new ice-cap in our library.

Please bring to school as much ice as you can. Also, keep it in something that will stop it from melting on the way or your lunch will get soggy. Also, don't tell anybody. If anybody asks why you have so much ice, just act normal.

Meet me in the library.

Jenny.

CHAPTER 5

I told Dad that Adam and I wanted oxtail stew for tea. This was because Dad had made lots of oxtail stew a long time ago, and we didn't like it, so Dad had put it into bags and frozen it.

When he got it out of the freezer, it made enough space for me to put in lots of plastic sandwich bags filled with water. I put them in just before bed so that he didn't notice.

In the morning, I packed them into my bag and Adam's bag, and we went to school. Before the bell rang, we snuck into the library.

We went right to the back of the maths section and put them in the cupboard. The cupboard is full of all the pipes to the school's heating, but it was not turned on, so it was nice and cold.

Sam arrived just after us, and gave us a cake-tin full of ice. Alfred came next. He had got two whole carrier bags full of ice, I don't know how. He must have a very big freezer, and his Mum must have got him to school without even noticing a bit.

By the time the bell went the whole cupboard was full of our new ice-cap and we had to put the last few bits of ice by the door and behind the bookcase. It was OK because it was very cold in the library.

The school day was all about our Christmas plays. Adam had to practise for his. He was playing an angel and he had to say, "I am here to show you the way to the stable!" in a very loud voice.

This is OK because Adam has a very loud voice anyway. If I had known what was going to happen, I would have told him to practise saying, "I am here to show you the way to escape!" instead, but I didn't.

I had art, and we were making the Santa's grotto for our play. It was a big cave, big enough to fit the whole class in when we sing our Christmas song, and it was decorated with tinsel and glitter, in blue and green and red and gold, and there are lots of paper chains. It was long and thin so that we could carry it across to the hall when we put the play on.

I told Mrs. Dribble, the art teacher, about the grotto in town and I said we should put plastic bags over ours to make it waterproof.

She said yes, because she likes it when we have our own artistic vision — which means doing things that are different from the way other people do them. I have my own artistic vision a lot.

We used a big green thick plastic sheet and we stuck Christmas tree bits on it and we hung coloured balls all over it.

At lunch time Adam and I went back to the library. Adam looked for people with ice. He kept saying, "I am here to show you the way to the ice-cap," so he could practise more for his play.

More and more people came in with ice until the whole Maths section and most of the Art section was filled with ice-cap.

Every day, I got people to bring in more ice, and by the end of the week I thought the plan to make a new ice-cap was going very well indeed.

But when we got into school on Monday, I found the plan had gone much, much too well, and to make matters worse, Monday was the day of the Christmas Play...

CHAPTER 6

Everybody was lining up to go into the school hall to watch the plays. It was not just all the children, but the parents as well. Dad was in the queue talking to all the other parents. They were mainly pointing at each other's babies and talking about which schools they wanted them to go to when they were older.

Mr. Grey from the council was also there to watch the plays. Mr. Grey comes to the school a lot – usually when strange things are happening. He doesn't like strange things happening and he usually tries to fix them. He is very bad at fixing things and usually makes them worse.

Today, his nose was red and he kept sniffing. He looked cold.

Adam's class play was going to be on first, and Adam was already in his angel costume. My play was going to be on last, and we were all supposed to go and get the big grotto and carry it into the hall when Adam's play had finished.

Adam and I decided to go and check on the ice cap before the play, so we crept away.

As we went past, I heard Mr. Grey say to Mrs. Dribble, "It's freezing in here!"

Mrs. Dribble said, "You don't give us enough money to have the heating on!" The council pays the money to run the school and the teachers are always saying there is not enough money to do things. That is why we had to stop building our space rocket, but that is in another story.

Mr. Grey said, "It's far too cold. Go and turn the heating on!" and I saw Mrs. Dribble going off to do it while Adam and I crept into the library.

The room was FREEZING because almost the whole library was ice-cap. You could see the books, but you couldn't read them because they were frozen into one big solid lump of ice that went from the back of the library to the front and from the floor right up to the ceiling.

This was good in one way because I was sure it would definitely save Christmas. But in another way, it was not good because somebody was bound to notice that the whole library was filled with ice.

There was a little space around the side of the ice-cap and Adam and I crawled in to see what had happened. I used a pen to dig a tunnel through the ice to the cupboard at the very back.

That's where I found that things were really bad.

Remember I said that the cupboard had all the heating pipes for the school in it? Well, the ice had broken them and water had come out. It must have been coming out all weekend, and then freezing into more and more ice.

It was not just the library, I could see where the ice had gone into the gap under the floor as well. The whole school must be filled with ice under the floors and inside the heating!

We crept back out, and we were just about to go into the hall when we heard a noise behind us.

It was a rattling, groaning, pouring sound. I knew what it was. It was the sound of the heating being turned on.

Then I had a very quick thought. It went like this:

- The heating pipes are broken behind the ice-cap.
- If the heating is turned on, hot water will come out instead of cold.

- The hot water will melt the ice-cap in the library.

This was bad and I only had about one second to think about how bad it was before I heard the most terribly loud crashing sound...

CHAPTER 7

I turned round just in time to see the doors of the library explode open and a wave of icy water pour out towards us.

It was like a waterfall coming out of the library filled with ice and wet books. It filled the corridor and rushed towards us.

"Look!" said Adam.

I grabbed him and we ran along the corridor. I could feel the splashes on my back as we ran and a copy of "The Cat in the Hat" hit me on the head.

I opened the first classroom door I could find, and pulled Adam inside. Then I slammed the door just in time, as a wall of water burst past outside.

A little bit of water dripped through the sides of the door, and it bulged out a bit, but it stayed shut.

Slowly the noise of the water got quieter, but that's when I knew there was a REALLY big problem.

The classroom door had a glass window, and when we looked out through it, I couldn't believe what I saw. The corridor outside was completely filled with water. There were books and papers and even a computer floating around out there.

Our ice cap had been huge, and now it had completely melted because the heating had been turned on. The whole school was now filled with water, and we were stuck!

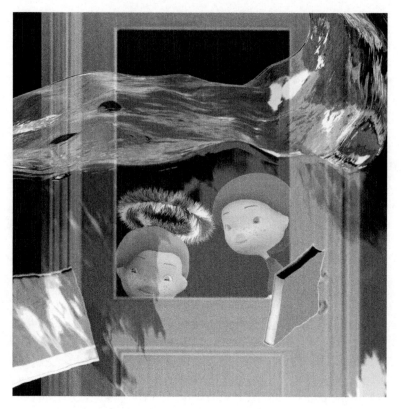

On the other side of the corridor, I could see through the big glass doors into the hall. None of the teachers or the kids or the parents had noticed, because Adam's

Christmas play had started and everyone was watching the stage.

The hall doors had stayed shut, so everyone inside was safe – as long as nobody opened the doors!

We now had three problems:

1) The school was full of water.
2) Adam was not in the hall, and so he would not be there to say, "I am here to show you the way to the stable" in the play.
3) The ice-cap had melted so Christmas would still be early.

Problem 3 was probably the worst problem, but I decided to fix problems 1 and 2 first, so I thought of a plan. I think of my best plans when things are really bad, and this was a very good one, but I knew it would be a bit wet if it went wrong.

Adam and I put a chair on top of a desk and I used it to hold him up to the ceiling.

Adam pushed the ceiling tiles out of the way (they are easy to move) and climbed up. Then I gave him a skipping rope which we found in one of the desks and he tied it to the roof so I could climb up too.

The space in the ceiling of the school is a bit dirty and full of spiders and paper darts, so Adam loved it.

We climbed along inside the ceiling until we got to the school hall. I could hear Adam's play going on underneath us and it was nearly at the bit where he would have to be an angel and say, "I am here to show you the way to the stable." Anyway, his angel costume was a bit wet and very dirty now.

I told Adam what my plan was, then I took one of the ceiling tiles out, and looked down through it.

I could see everyone watching the play. I could see the manger with the baby in it. (It was not a real baby. We used a doll with a halo made of tinsel and one of its arms was missing.)

Also, I could see the wise men and the shepherds. They were looking a bit lost because there was nobody there to show them the way to the stable and they were waiting for an angel. Also, Dad was looking around to see where Adam was, and so was Adam's teacher.

I got the skipping rope and tied it round Adam, then I lowered him through the hole so that he was hanging above the stage.

Nobody had seen such good flying from an angel in a school play before and everybody clapped.

Adam said, "I am here to show you the way to escape!" in a very loud voice.

Adam's teacher whispered, "The STABLE –
I am here to show you the way to THE
STABLE!" because she thought he had got it
wrong, but Adam carried on.

"The school is full of water," he said, and he
pointed to the doors where there was a bit of
water coming through, and some desks were
floating past outside.

The parents and the teachers looked round
and started to get a bit worried because now
they knew it wasn't part of the play.

Adam said, "Stay in the hall. Me and my sister
are going to get a submarine." Then I pulled
him back up.

People were running around shouting at each other in the hall. Then Dad stood up and said, "Everybody calm down!"

Then he said, "If Jenny and Adam say they are getting a submarine, then we should just wait for the submarine." He said it as if waiting for a submarine was what you did in all school Christmas plays.

This was Dad Acting Normal.

CHAPTER 8

I led Adam back inside the ceiling of the classrooms. I knew where I wanted to take us, but I wasn't sure how to get there.

The first time I pulled back a ceiling tile to look at where we were, all I could see was water. It was so high that I could almost touch it by reaching through the ceiling.

I lowered Adam down into the water so he could tell me where we were. He splashed about a bit, hanging on the rope, and then stuck his head underwater. Then he swam down into the water.

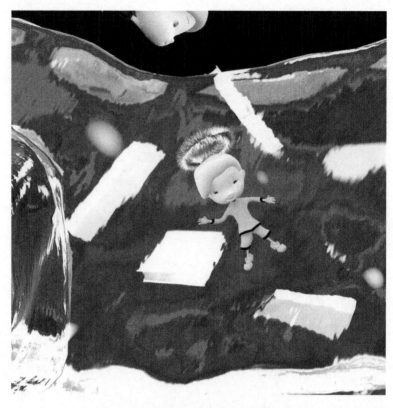

when he came up he was holding a copy of "Charlie and the Chocolate Factory." That meant we were in the library. I knew the books were in order with the writers starting with A at the front and Z at the back. "Charlie and the Chocolate Factory" is by

Roald Dahl, so that meant we must be at the front of the library in the 'D' section.

I pulled Adam up and we crawled on. When I opened the ceiling again, and lowered Adam down, he swam away again. This time he came back with "Gangsta Granny" which is by David Walliams, so I knew we were nearly at the end of the library, in the 'W' section.

We crawled on even further, and then I said, "Stop!" I really hoped there would be no water when I pulled back the next ceiling tile.

We were in luck. We had got the right classroom which was the Art room, and the door must have been shut when the school flooded. There was only a little puddle of water on the floor, and most of that was coming from Adam who was very soggy. He had soggy hair, and a soggy shirt and soggy pants.

Remember how I said my class were making a Santa's Grotto? And remember I said it was big enough for everyone to stand in it? And remember I got them to make it waterproof?

Well, all we had to do was tie some see-through plastic sheet down over the front and we had a sort of submarine!

Adam and I got into our Santa's submarine grotto, and lifted it up from the inside. We walked it over to the classroom door.

I reached through the plastic sheet and opened the door. We were almost washed off our feet and into the back of the classroom. The whole room filled with very cold water very quickly.

The bottom of our submarine was open so the icy water flowed around our ankles and through the plastic we could see everything from the Art room floating around. But the water was kept from filling up the grotto.

It was like turning a bowl upside down in the bath. The air was trapped inside with us. I had seen this done before on TV with a diving bell, but I had never seen it done with a Santa's grotto.

The tinsel floated around us like seaweed and the coloured Christmas balls hung upwards instead of down because they were full of air. It was a very Christmassy submarine.

Slowly, we walked with our submarine along the corridor until we got to the hall doors.

This was the tricky bit...

CHAPTER 9

Everyone inside the hall was a bit scared. Mrs. Dribble and Dad were trying to keep them calm by getting the kids to sing Christmas songs.

We could hear "Away in a Manger" coming from inside the hall, but it sounded a bit bubbly because we were underwater.

We had to put the front of the Santa submarine grotto right over the hall doors so no water could get in at the sides. Then I lifted up the plastic, and opened the door. It was like an air-lock.

Adam went inside in his very wet, dirty angel costume and said, in a voice that was much louder than the singing, "I am here to show you the way into the submarine."

Everybody queued up at the door (we are very good at queueing up in our school – we do it a lot) and they all got into our Santa submarine grotto. Then I pulled down the plastic in front of the doors.

It was very crowded and I started to worry about how much air there was in the submarine.

We all walked slowly down the corridor with Santa's grotto around us and books from the library floating about outside. Somebody started singing "Away in a Manger" again and everyone joined in as we shuffled along with our feet in the cold water.

When we got to the big doors at the front of the school, we couldn't open them. I thought we would be stuck, but Adam told us to step back.

Then he said to run, and we all ran at the doors. When we hit them, the grotto broke open, but so did the doors, and we all popped out really fast into the playground with all the water whooshing out behind us and pushing us along, until all the parents and the teachers and the children ended up in a big wet tangled pile in the car park.

CHAPTER 10

And that's how the North Pole came to our school library, Santa's Grotto was turned into a submarine and everybody was rescued by a little angel.

When I told Dad about the ice-cap and showed him my Maths, he said we had better have a long talk about Santa Claus. He told me a big secret (which I'm not going to tell you) about Santa and how all the presents get to all the children in time for Christmas. It's really, really clever. It's even cleverer than the rocket sled I thought he must use.

In the end, Christmas didn't come early. It came at exactly the right time, and our stockings were full on Christmas morning.

I still think quite a lot about what the Santa in the town said to me, though. He asked me whether I'd been good or bad.

I still don't really know because I did fill the school with water, and ruin the play, but I was trying to save Christmas, and I did rescue everyone in the end.

I think the only thing to do is TRY to be good, and if it all goes wrong, just keep trying until something works.

The End.

Act Normal and read more...

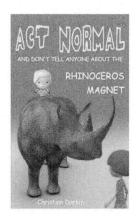

Printed in Great Britain
by Amazon